BENNY BENSKY

AND THE PEROGY PALACE

BENNY BENSKY
AND THE PEROGY PALACE

by Mary Borsky

Illustrations by Linda Hendry

Tundra Books

Published in Canada by Tundra Books, *McClelland & Stewart Young Readers*,
481 University Avenue, Toronto, Ontario M5G 2E9

Published in the United States by Tundra Books of Northern New York,
P.O. Box 1030, Plattsburgh, New York 12901

Library of Congress Catalog Number: 00-135462

Canadian Cataloguing in Publication Data
Borsky, Mary, 1946-
    Benny Bensky and the Perogy Palace
ISBN 0-88776-523-8
I. Hendry, Linda.   II. Title.

PS8553.O735B46 2001   jC813'.54   C00-932282-5
PZ7.B67Be 2001

We acknowledge the support of the Canada Council for the Arts and the
Ontario Arts Council for our publishing program.

ONTARIO ARTS COUNCIL
CONSEIL DES ARTS DE L'ONTARIO

We acknowledge the financial support of the Government of Canada
through the Book Publishing Industry Development Program for our
publishing activities.

Design by Ingrid Paulson
Printed and bound in Canada

1 2 3 4 5 6   06 05 04 03 02 01

For Julia
M. B.

For Babcia
L. H.

CONTENTS

One Simple Thing

Benny Bensky was not a dog who usually dug the dirt out of the plants in the living room. In fact, he hardly ever did. Not unless his owner, Rosie, was occupied with something else – her bottle cap collection, for example – as she was now. Not unless Rosie's parents, Mr. and Mrs. Bensky, were in the other room, as they were at the moment. And even then, not unless it was an extra special occasion, as this one was. Nine-year-old Rosie had just finished grade four (no more pencils, no more books . . . !), and this was her first day of summer holidays.

Summer holidays! Benny thought, scooping up the soil from around the roots of the home-grown avocado and kicking it energetically across the blue rug. *Summer holidays at last! Summer holidays at very,* very *long last!*

And he was so jubilant, so celebratory, so filled with high hopes, that when he finished digging out the avocado, he started on the potted palm.

All winter, Benny'd had to stay at home by himself while Rosie was at school and Mr. and Mrs. Bensky were at work at the Perogy Palace. But now it was summer, and the fun, Benny told himself, was about to begin!

Benny threw himself full length on the blue rug, rolled his furry black body vigorously in the unpotted soil, then snorted his rubbery black nose as he inhaled the fragrant summery smells of the soft earth. Finally, relaxed and refreshed, he sighed, stretched out his furry black legs, and touched his black front toes lightly against Rosie's bare legs.

"Eleven DAD'S Root Beer," Rosie said, bending her curly head down toward her collection. She was lying on the rug too, completely absorbed in the enjoyable holiday chore of sorting and stacking her bottle caps. "Thirteen, no, fourteen Dr Pepper, nine Grape Crush."

Benny Bensky was a large dog – longer than Rosie when he was stretched out beside her, and wider too. He had floppy black ears, a long black tail, and a large eraser-like black nose. He was completely black. Except, that is, for his caramel-colored eyebrows, which gave him the look of a dog with something on his mind, and except for a dusting of white under his chin, which gave him the look of a dog who'd just eaten something tasty.

Rosie reached back to stroke Benny's velvety black muzzle, and Benny breathed a long contented sigh. Rosie smiled.

"Benny knows it's summer holidays," Rosie called to her mother, who was in the kitchen. "Isn't he smart, Mum? Isn't he wonderful? Isn't he the best dog in the world?"

"He's a good boy, our Benny," called Mrs. Bensky from the kitchen table, where she and Mr. Bensky were drinking their morning coffee. She wiggled her shiny red fingernails in the doorway. "Clever doggie-woggie."

Benny thumped his tail once against the blue rug. Then, still pressing his muzzle to Rosie's hand, he closed his eyes and listened contentedly to the homey sounds of toast popping from the toaster, of coffee percolating in its pot, of Mr. Bensky stretching, cracking his knuckles, then yawning loudly. He heard Mrs. Bensky pad to the side door closet, where Benny knew she was slipping on her clickety red heels and zipping on her puffy white perogy costume.

Mrs. Bensky dressed as a walking, talking perogy when she went to work at the Perogy Palace, where she seated customers, brought them menus, and offered them samples of different types of perogies to choose from.

Mr. Bensky worked in the kitchen, where he wore a white cook's jacket with the words *Perogy Palace* embroidered in blue on the front. His job was to roll out the dough for the perogies, to stuff them with cheese or potatoes or mushrooms, then to boil them and drizzle them with butter for the customers at the front.

"Perogies are the food of champions!" he liked to explain to Rosie's friends. "Taste the soft buttery dumpling! Taste the flavorful and satisfying cheese and potato filling! You want a different kind of filling? You want meat? You want mushroom? You want, maybe, strawberry? I can make any kind of filling you want." And he heaped their plates high with different types of perogies to sample. "Here. Eat with plenty of butter and sour cream. Eat in good health! Eat! Eat!"

"You know how Benny's always so worried when I'm going to school, Mum?" Rosie called from the living room rug. "How his eyebrows ping-pong back and forth? His eyebrows aren't ping-ponging at all today! He's not the least bit worried. He can tell I'm staying home! Today, he's totally mellow!"

"Now, that's just excellent!" her mother answered from the kitchen.

"Aren't you glad you let me keep him?" Rosie continued. "Aren't you glad we didn't leave him outside all alone in the cold? Aren't you glad we have a dog like Benny?"

"Delighted," answered Mr. Bensky in a flat, ironical tone. "One hundred percent delighted."

Mellow, thought Benny to himself. *Mellow*.

The word echoed in his doggie brain as he lay sprawled, belly side down, on the soil-fragrant blue rug. He sighed and wiggled his muscular shoulders even more deeply into the thick pile of the rug. *Mellow. Marshmallow.*

Benny had heard the word 'marshmallow' from Rosie. And what a wonderful word it was! Rosie had told him about campfires too, and tents and sleeping bags and owls and loons and how they would go camping when summer holidays came and how

much fun they would have and how they would love it.

I can practically smell marshmallows, Benny thought dreamily. *There is no school. It is summer holidays. I feel as if I am lying beside the campfire inhaling the fine summery aroma of leaves, wood smoke, hot dogs, and toasting marshmallows. Rosie is toasting a row of marshmallows over the embers, and I know she will give the very first one to me.* And Benny thought of the plump, toasty marshmallow, cooled to perfection for him.

My back feels cozy from the campfire, Benny thought. *Yet my face is fresh from the cooling night breeze. Why listen, somewhere an owl is calling!*

"Who knows? Who knows?" Mr. Bensky could be heard saying to his wife in the kitchen. "Who knows why? Who?"

There was a clink of cutlery, then Mr. Bensky spoke again. "But I can see for myself that business is slow in the Perogy Palace. Business is awful slow. Even with our prime downtown location. Even with the nice big picture windows. Even with the brand-new blue neon sign that says PEROGY PALACE."

"I've been wondering," said Mrs. Bensky. "Maybe people don't know what a perogy is."

"Were people smarter a month ago?" Mr. Bensky asked. "A month ago, no one in the entire town of Smith Falls had a problem remembering what a perogy was. A month ago, we had a full house."

"Maybe we should have sold the Perogy Palace a month ago. Maybe we should have sold it when we had a buyer. There was that woman calling all the time asking to buy it, remember?"

"Sell the very building Grandpa Bensky built as a bowling alley back in the fifties? No! Never! Sell a prize restaurant like ours? I don't think so! We've got to hang in a little longer. We're not going down without a fight!"

"You're right. You're absolutely right," Mrs. Bensky replied. "The Perogy Palace is not just *any* building! It's been in the family for two generations now. Why, it's a heritage building! We can't let it go. You're right, dear. We'll find a way to get through this." She was silent, then, after a moment, quietly added one more word: "Somehow."

The sound of their conversation came to Benny from far away, like distant voices from a tent on the far side of the campsite. How he loved humans, Benny thought. How he loved his human family! Dogs always said that humans were a dog's best friend, and it was true.

"Billy Bittle the Barber doesn't come by for a mid-morning dish of perogies like he used to," Mr. Bensky said sadly. "And do you notice how Molly the Mail Carrier just drops off the mail and rushes off. She doesn't stand around and hint for samples like she used to." Mr. Bensky sighed. "Why, even our own *dog* won't eat them anymore."

"Benny Bensky? *Our* Benny?" Mrs. Bensky protested. "Why, Benny *loves* your perogies, dear. I'm sure of it."

"Not anymore he doesn't."

Benny raised his ear slightly when he heard his name being spoken in the distance, then flopped it down again. Benny loved his human family, but he loved the little human – Rosie – best. The full-grown humans – Mr. and Mrs. Bensky – were very nice, but full-grown humans, Benny'd noticed, were rarely as playful or cuddly as the little ones.

"Benny *does* love your perogies, dear," Mrs. Bensky's voice could be heard saying. "I know he does. Here, I'll prove it." And there was the muffled clunk of someone opening the fridge, the rattle of a dish, the poof of a plastic container being opened.

"Benny!" Mrs. Bensky called invitingly. "Ben-ny!"

From the far side of the campsite in his imagination, Benny could hear someone singing his name. Benny smiled to himself as he dozed. How he loved to hear his name in a song.

But suddenly, without warning, a shiver shook Benny's sturdy body. There seemed to be a sudden chill, a totally new briskness in the air. Benny wiggled his nose. There was a new smell as well – something strange, something ominous, something he couldn't quite place. Why, a menacing presence seemed to have entered the bright circle of his campfire.

"BENNY BENSKY!" the menacing presence thundered, "WHAT HAVE YOU DONE NOW? YOU DUMB, USELESS, GOOD-FOR-NOTHING MUTT!!"

Cautiously, Benny opened one eye and was startled to see Mr. Bensky's red angry face looming over him and the fragrant soil that was spread over the blue living room rug. Beside him stood Mrs. Bensky dressed as a perogy, holding a smaller real perogy on a saucer in front of her, her face crumpled into a look of shock and dismay.

In one furious scramble, Benny Bensky flung himself to his feet and jumped up to give Mrs. Bensky's face a consoling lick. Then seeing Mr. Bensky's face again, Benny wagged his entire hindquarters in such wild apology that he sent the saucer spinning from Mrs. Bensky's hands and across the living room.

The saucer bounced off the door frame, flipping the buttery perogy up against the flowered wallpaper in the hallway. The perogy held to the wall for a moment, before it plopped to the floor beside the hall rug. The saucer rolled across the floor, clunked into the telephone table, then spun like a coin before it stopped.

There was a stunned silence in the room.

Presently, there was a tap at the front screened door. "Rosie! Are you home? Rosie! Want to play?" a girl's voice called. It was Fran, Rosie's friend.

Everyone was still too stunned to speak.

Finally Fran poked her head inside the screened door. It was then that she saw the dirt on the rug, the perogy on the hall floor, the saucer by the telephone stand, and the four Benskys standing motionless in the middle of it all.

"Uh-oh," Fran said, taking everything in. She slipped inside to stand beside Rosie.

Finally Mr. Bensky opened his mouth.

"Dirt all over the blue rug," Mr. Bensky said in a choked voice. "Our fine potted palm, our tender avocado, bare-rooted in their pots! Butter on the new flowered wallpaper! Look, even the corners of the cushions on the couch are chewed off!"

"The corners of the cushions aren't from today, dear," said Mrs. Bensky. "He chewed the corners off the cushions last week." She plugged in the vacuum cleaner.

Fran pulled Benny off the rug and held him by his collar while Mrs. Bensky vacuumed the dirt from the rug. Mr. Bensky examined the bare-rooted plants and wiped off the dirt that had flown up on top of the coffee table. Rosie picked up the saucer, then gathered her scattered bottle caps.

"What about the wall?" demanded Mr. Bensky, when the vacuum cleaner finally went off. "What about the perogy?"

"Benny'll clean up the perogy, Daddy," Rosie interjected quickly. "Benny'll eat it."

Mrs. Bensky finished wiping the wall with a wet cloth. "Benny'd *love* to eat that perogy," she said. "Wouldn't you, Benny?" Her puffy white perogy outfit crinkled.

"Eat it, Benny," said Rosie.

"Eat it, Benny," said Fran.

"Good boy, Benny," smiled Mrs. Bensky. She kissed the air with her lipsticked lips and wiggled her eyebrows encouragingly. "Come on, Benny. Eat it."

Benny took a quick sideways glance at the perogy (which used to be his favorite human food), shifted a little farther away from it, and looked up at the ceiling.

"Eat it, you dumb mutt," yelled Mr. Bensky, taking Benny by the collar and steering him in the direction of the perogy.

Benny gave his tail a brief apologetic half-wag, then stared in the opposite direction, his brown eyebrows crunched close together.

"See?" said Mr. Bensky sadly. "I told you. No one will eat my perogies anymore. *No one*."

"Don't be too hard on him, dear," said Mrs. Bensky. "He's only a pup."

"Who's paying the bills around here, if I may be so bold as to ask?" thundered Mr. Bensky. He glared at Benny. "Who's putting a roof over this mutt's head? Who's keeping his dish filled with premium-grade doggie kibble? Not to mention, who brought him in out of the freezing rain and saved his life?"

"Fran and I were the ones who did that, Daddy," Rosie said. "We were the ones who brought him in. Only it wasn't freezing rain, it was just freezing cold."

"But I remember he was covered with icicles!" said Rosie's father. "I remember that was part of the high-powered sales pitch – 'Look, Daddy! He's freezing! He's covered in icicles!'"

"Somehow he'd gotten wet," agreed Mrs. Bensky. "But no, it was below zero that day, so it couldn't have been raining."

"Still," Mr. Bensky said. "I was the one who broke down! I was the one who took pity! I was the one who *allowed* you to bring him in out of the cold!" He thumped his hand against his heart. "Wasn't I? I want to set the record straight here."

"Yes, Daddy," Rosie said, giving him a hug. "You *were* the one."

"You did a wonderful thing that day, Mr. Bensky," Fran said.

"Thank you," said Mr. Bensky. "Thank you for that small but important piece of recognition. I was, indeed, instrumental in saving this dog's life."

"Oh, absolutely!" said Mrs. Bensky.

Mr. Bensky smiled modestly, then turned and glowered at Benny and the uneaten perogy. "Yet this same dog refuses now to comply with one simple, simple, *simple* request."

Rosie and Fran knelt beside Benny and put their arms around him. Benny hung his head in shame.

"He ate the gas bill last week," added Mr. Bensky. "He chewed the toes right out of my favorite pair of orange socks. Plus, just yesterday, I had a nice freshly glazed maple-walnut doughnut on the edge of the bathtub . . . climbed in for a nice, relaxing soak, and when I reached for my doughnut, it was gone! Not a crumb left! This dumb dog had devoured it in a single bite!"

"All of it?" asked Mrs. Bensky.

"He'll learn, Mr. Bensky." Fran said quickly.

"Oh, yes! He'll learn, Daddy." Rosie added.

"He will," agreed Mrs. Bensky. "I'm sure he'll learn at some point."

"Darn tootin'!" said Mr. Bensky. "Darn tootin', he'll learn!" He strode to the hallway, flipped through the phone book, tapped in a number, and began to speak.

"Dog obedience school?" he said. "Oh, good. Listen. I got a dog here, pretty short on obedience, not to mention the brains department."

Obedience school! Benny registered, and sat bolt upright.

"Obedience school?" Rosie said, standing up beside Benny.

"Obedience school?" Fran said, standing up on the other side of Benny.

Mrs. Bensky looked around at the bare-rooted plants, at the rug, at the cushions with their corners chewed off. She looked at Benny. "Maybe it *is* about the right time for obedience school," she said thoughtfully.

"Totally individualized programs? Scientifically tested methods?" Mr. Bensky was shouting into the phone. "Music to my ears! Listen, the dog is dumb, but I'm desperate. He digs plants out of their pots right in the living room! He chews the corners off cushions! He chews toes out of socks! He also ate my doughnut right off the edge of the bathtub. Plus, when I have some small request – some totally *simple* thing – he refuses! He won't even consider it! I tell you, it's the absolute last straw!"

Mr. Bensky turned around to scowl at Benny, who was sitting between Rosie and Fran, his eyes downcast, his shoulders slouched.

"Tomorrow?" Mr. Bensky continued. "Absolutely. Tomorrow is perfect. We'll be there at 9:00 A.M. sharp, Ms. Viola Pin. Believe me, we'll be there."

Ms. Viola Pin! Benny jolted upright, the hairs on the back of his neck rising slightly. He knew Ms. Viola Pin, whose house they passed every day on their way to the tree fort in the park. He knew Ms. Viola Pin, whose house he'd first seen that day he wandered – cold, lonely, lost, and bewildered – when he was no more than a tiny pup.

"Ms. Viola Pin!" cried Rosie. "Ms. Viola Pin is mean, Daddy! She stares at us from behind her hedge!"

"She says we touch her flowers!" said Fran.

"She says our singing scares her cat!" said Rosie.

"She won't let us chalk a hopscotch on the sidewalk beside her house!" added Fran.

"Everyone's scared of her, Daddy!" said Rosie.

"Even Benny pulls the opposite way if he sees her in her yard!"

"She never claimed to be running a charm school," Rosie's father countered. "She's running a dog obedience school."

But, thought Benny, shivering a little. He thought of Ms. Viola Pin's sharp and glittery eyes, her scissory face. *But. . .*

"But, Daddy . . .," implored Rosie.

"But it's summer holidays!" said Fran.

"Good manners don't have a season," said Mr. Bensky. He gazed into the distance and smiled faintly to himself, rolling up to the balls of his feet and down again as he spoke. "We need good manners in every season, in every weather, at every hour of the day. Manners are the grease on the squeaky axle of life! Manners are that nice, neat little cardboard container that holds your french fries! Manners are, if you will, the handy hooks where we hang our jackets!"

At this, he straightened his back, rubbed his hands briskly, then took his Perogy Palace jacket from its hook in the closet. He leaned down to Rosie and cheerfully kissed her good-bye.

"You certainly have given us food for thought, dear," said Mrs. Bensky as she straightened the collar of his cook's uniform. She put her arms around Rosie and kissed her, hugged Fran too, then left with Mr. Bensky for work in the Perogy Palace.

Through the screened window, Benny could hear them as they continued their conversation.

"Do you think a new paint-job might pick up business at the Perogy Palace?" asked Mr. Bensky. "Or how about a nice striped awning for the front entrance?"

Benny turned to the spot where the perogy had landed. Maybe he would eat it after all, he thought. He sniffed the spot where the perogy had been.

There was still the faintest smell of butter on the wood floor, but the perogy itself was gone. Completely gone. Someone had cleared it away. Filled with remorse, Benny licked the spot on the floor where the perogy had been.

"Poor Benny!" Rosie said to Fran.

"Poor Benny!" Fran echoed, her words still echoing her disbelief.

Benny flopped to his belly on the cool kitchen floor. He lay as motionless as a black bear rug.

What is going to become of me? he asked himself. *Ms. Viola Pin? Ms. Viola Pin's Dog Obedience School?* He covered his eyes with his furry paws.

Not one Speck of Trouble

Benny Bensky poked his nose between the slats on the tree fort in the park and sighed.

Beneath him the grass was green. The sun sparked on the river, the birds sang, the squirrels navigated from branch to branch. In the river, a fish jumped for joy (No schools! No schools!).

But for Benny, everything was different. For Benny, there was a big, black, water balloon hanging over everything. Tomorrow he wouldn't be able to come to the tree fort in the park with Rosie and her best friend, Fran. Tomorrow he wouldn't be able to scan for cats, or scare squirrels, or ambush ducks. Tomorrow he wouldn't be able to sniff at grasses, snap at hornets, or feel the muddy river bank squish between his toes. Tomorrow he would no longer be a free citizen on the streets of Smith Falls. Benny's heart felt exactly like a ruined, ragged, mushed up, moldy, waterlogged old tennis ball.

Tomorrow, Benny told himself, *I will be in school. In Ms. Viola Pin's Dog Obedience School!*

School, Benny thought. The word echoed across his mind like a howl over a dark and lonely lake. *Schooooool!*

"School's not that bad, Benny," Rosie said, reading his mind. Her eyes looked troubled, though, as she pulled burrs from his black coat.

"No," smiled Fran, shaking out her black hair then snapping it back into a ponytail with a colored elastic she had around her wrist. She was the same age as Rosie, in the same class in school, and could always get Rosie to laugh. "School's not that *that* bad."

"Or even that that *that* bad," said Rosie, bravely attempting a smile of her own.

Rosie massaged Benny's head and ears, and Fran massaged his back and belly. Benny closed his eyes and tried to remember back to happier times, to the very first time he'd ever been in this tree fort.

Well, perhaps those were not exactly happy times, Benny thought, shifting to a more comfortable position on the plywood floor. His first visit to the tree fort had occurred during what could be more accurately described as interesting times.

What Benny remembered was being a small puppy – cold, abandoned, afraid, all by himself – on the streets of Smith Falls.

"Good luck, kid," a voice said, and a hand pushed him from the warm truck onto the cold street. The truck door slammed in his startled face, the engine revved, then the truck sped off, leaving Benny standing and staring, not able to make any sense out of what was happening.

It was a blustery gray day, with a few flakes of white blowing down from the sky. There were many houses, more than he'd ever seen before, rows of them, all with their doors shut. There were gray roads criss-crossing in every direction, and so much coldness in the air.

Very soon, the cold and damp of the pavement seeped into Benny's toes. He tucked his head and tail down against the wind and walked quickly in the direction the truck had gone. Or – then, again –

had it gone the other way? Benny walked quickly in the opposite direction, but both directions looked exactly the same. He turned around and went still another way.

Presently, he found himself beside a river and among many huge, leafless trees. From the branches of a cluster of ancient willows, he saw two girls laughing and pointing.

"A puppy!" the girls were saying. "Oh, look! A little black puppy!" And they scrambled eagerly from the branches above him. Green polar-fleeced arms embraced him from the front. Purple polar-fleeced arms embraced him from the back.

"Isn't he sweet, Rosie!" the purple-jacketed girl said.

"I think he's lost, Fran," the green-jacketed girl answered.

They led him up a sturdy slanted willow trunk to a small tree fort half-hidden in the branches of the massive willows. Benny wagged his tail and licked their faces. But unable to forget his troubles, he soon struggled free from their arms, made his way down the huge willow trunk, and continued on his journey.

Where was his owner? His home? His warm truck? Benny's caramel-colored eyebrows were knotted tight with worry as he walked hurriedly along, through one back alley, across a front yard, up a busy street.

Big black wheels ripped through the air beside his shoulder, and a horn blared in his ear. "Hey!" a taxi driver yelled. "Watch where you're going!"

"Not in here, you don't!" a woman said when Benny looked longingly into the open door of a heated van.

"Go home!" a man yelled as he placed two plastic bags of garbage at the curb.

Then suddenly Benny saw something that made his spirits lift. He saw an open door and inviting yellow light inside – the look of warmth and welcome and shelter. He ran hopefully up the steps and through the open door. But instantly a broom snapped down through the air in front of him, stinging his nose.

"Out of here! OUT! OUT! OUT!" a woman's voice shrieked. The red-haired woman dressed in black chased him out into the yard, flailing her broom after him. She grabbed the hose from the side of her house, turned its cold spray on Benny, and laughed aloud.

From the woman's lighted window, a white cat smirked.

Stunned, Benny tried his best to shake himself, but some of the water had already frozen to his skin

and fur, stinging his ears and forming ice crystals between his toes.

Where was there a place to warm himself? Where was there a place to lie down?

Limping now, and exhausted from the cold, Benny wandered farther down the street.

"It's that same black puppy, Fran!" he heard a girl's voice call. "He really *is* lost!"

"Why, he's got icicles in his fur!"

"He's cold and shivering!"

"We've got to get him inside, Rosie!"

"We've got to dry him off!"

"We've got to feed him!"

"We've got to play with him!"

"We've got to . . . got to . . . *keep* him!" Both girls laughed.

When Benny awoke later, cozy and warm on a fleecy blanket inside a cardboard box, he heard human voices.

"Because dogs have *dog germs*, that's why not," he heard a rumbly man's voice saying. "Because dogs have *dog hair*. Because dogs leave *dog prints*. Anyway, what's wrong with Fran's house? Why don't Fran's parents keep him?"

"My mum and dad have allergies, Mr. Bensky," a girl's voice answered.

"Smooth move," the man replied. "That shows considerable foresight on their part." There was the sound of popcorn popping in its popper, the smell of butter melting. "You'll have to call the animal shelter, girls. I'm sorry."

"But the animal shelter is already crowded, Daddy!" a girl's voice said.

"Still, it's his best hope," a woman said. "I'm sorry too, girls, but it's the only way."

Benny listened dozily from his warm blanket. He wasn't paying attention to the actual words, but to some easy and comfortable flow beneath them. He liked this place he'd found. He liked the humans here. This place felt good and right. This place felt like . . . well . . . it felt like *home*.

He stretched, gave a little yip of a yawn, then stood up on his back legs, resting his furry front paws on the edge of the box. He grinned up at all the humans, thumped his tail energetically against the side of the box, and eagerly watched while smiles bloomed on all their faces.

"He *has* been as good as gold all afternoon," the woman admitted, bending down to pat him.

"You'd never find a better puppy!" the girl called Rosie said with feeling.

"Look at it this way, Mr. Bensky," the girl called Fran said sensibly. "You have a unique opportunity. You have the opportunity to save this puppy's life!"

There was a silence as the girls buried their faces in Benny's soft black puppy fur.

"He could be Rosie's Christmas present, Mr.

Bensky!" Fran said, looking up suddenly. "Your shopping would all be done!"

"Oh, please Daddy!" Rosie begged. "*Please!* It would be the best Christmas of my life!"

"I have only got one thing to say," the man called Mr. Bensky said after a long pause. He pointed to baby Benny. "He better not be one single *speck* of trouble!"

"He won't be! I promise! Oh, never!" the girls chorused.

"School is school," Rosie said now to Benny and Fran inside the tree fort. Benny opened his eyes a fraction of a moment. Rosie and Fran's faces looked slightly orange under the orange ground sheet that served as the tree fort's roof. "School is school is school. That's all."

"There's recess," Fran pointed out.

"Professional Development days!"

"Teachers' strikes!"

"Sometimes you get to erase the blackboard."

"Once I got picked to help in kindergarten and got to miss spelling," Fran said proudly.

"You missed spelling?"

"I had to do it for homework."

"Still," said Rosie, clearly impressed.

"My mum gets me a haircut at the hairdresser's when I start school," Fran said.

"Me too," said Rosie, brightening. "One time my mum bought me a Catwoman T-shirt."

Benny opened one eye at the word 'cat' and scanned the horizon. The girls laughed.

Rosie and Fran examined the pink mark on Benny's nose where a raccoon had scratched him. They ran their hands over his dusty coat and discovered a splatter of mud across one flank. They noticed the grime on his collar. They registered an odd fishy smell behind one ear and on his belly. Rosie turned up one of Benny's paws, and Fran turned up the other one. River mud was caked between his toes. They looked at each other.

"B-A-T-H," they spelled together. Then, laughing, they hooked baby fingers (which is what best friends do when they speak the same words at the same time) and said together: "Smoke goes up the chimney!"

So Soft and So Handsome

The floor of the Bensky bathroom was carpeted with towels. Bottles of every shape and color lined the sink and window ledge – VITA-GROW, CURLS 'N' SHINE, TWO-MINUTE HAIR REPAIR, DR. TONG'S SCALP RENEWER, WACKY WATERMELON SHAMPOO (in a watermelon-shaped bottle), and even OLD SPICE AFTERSHAVE.

A forlorn Benny Bensky stood up to his knees in bubbly water, his tail dripping, as suds foamed up around his drooping ears.

Rosie rinsed him clean with the detachable shower-head, then allowed him out of the tub. Benny braced himself, shook vigorously, then made a wild dash for Mr. and Mrs. Bensky's bed, where he planned to roll himself dry. But Fran was prepared, caught him in a giant bath towel, rubbed him down, and both girls took turns drying him with the hair dryer.

Sadly, Benny resigned himself to these indignities. The heady scent of the river, the tantalizing smell of the dead snake he'd rolled in, the alluring doggie fragrances he'd lingered over – all of it, he realized, was gone, gone, gone.

"You're so soft, Benny!" the girls exclaimed at intervals. "You're so handsome!" They were genuinely delighted over the difference the bath had made. "You look like a gentleman already, Benny!"

"Now you're ready for school," Rosie said happily. "You're ready to put your best foot forward!"

"Remember," Fran said, "Always sit straight and face the front."

"Listen carefully." Rosie urged.

"Do exactly what the teacher says."

"If there's a fire drill, line up and walk out in single file."

"No running."

"Lift your paw if you want to go to the bathroom."

"Stand tall for *O Canada!*."

Their instructions swirled in Benny's mind, leaving him slightly dizzy. Walk in single file? Face the front? Lift a paw? Stand tall? How would he ever remember all of it?

"You'll learn, Benny," Rosie said encouragingly.

"That's right, Benny," Fran said. "Everyone has to learn."

And because Benny looked so fine and so hand-some, and because it was summer holidays, and because the robins were singing, they snapped on Benny's leash and took him for a walk.

Twice, Benny tried to chase a cat, and three times he tried to roll in neighbors' flower gardens, but Rosie and Fran dug their heels in hard and held tightly to his leash.

"We're getting Benny ready for dog obedience school!" they explained to neighbors and passersby.

"Good luck!" Molly the Mail Carrier offered.

"Good going!" Billy Bittle the Barber replied.

"It's about time!" Rosie's neighbor, grumpy Mr. Gormley, called out from behind his newspaper.

Rosie and Fran and Benny walked two blocks to the bank machine where a sign read: "ATTENTION: FOR YOUR SECURITY YOU ARE BEING VIDEOTAPED." They stood in front of the camera, waved, then made up a song that they sang, watching themselves on the color monitor:

Benny Bensky is ready for school,
Benny Bensky is radically cool.
He's handsome and he's shiny,

And he's soft and he's clean.

Benny Bensky is the dog of my dreams!

Still practising their new song, they walked two blocks farther to the Perogy Palace, where they sang the song and danced the little dance for Mr. and Mrs. Bensky, who laughed and clapped.

"I can't believe the difference!" Mrs. Bensky exclaimed, admiring Benny's soft and shiny coat. "He positively glows! Are you sure you cleaned up the towels on the floor?"

"Great going, girls," Mr. Bensky said. "Great going." He looked troubled, though, as he turned toward the heaps of steaming perogies. He frowned a moment at the perogies, but didn't offer the girls any the way he usually did. "Why don't you get yourselves some french fries from the chip-wagon?" he said quietly, then opened the cash register and gave them each two dollars.

On the way back home, Rosie and Fran detoured through Vito's Videos where, as usual, Benny pulled them directly to the cash register, then put his front paws on the counter. Then, as always, Vito reached into his special jar of bone-marrow treats, gave one to Benny and said, "Hello there, handsome."

4

Bonne chance!

Benny Bensky woke to the delicate aroma of bacon and the sense that this was not a regular day. *Could it possibly be,* he asked himself dreamily, *Christmas morning?* He sniffed the air and wiggled himself slowly into wakefulness. *Could it possibly be,* he asked himself again, *my birthday? Could it possibly be . . .* and suddenly he opened his eyes to find Mr. Bensky beaming down at him.

"Good morning, Benny!" Mr. Bensky boomed. "All ready for your first day of obedience school?"

He chuckled as he assembled his fried egg and bacon sandwich.

Benny shook his head vigorously, flapping his ears. *Obedience school!* Now he remembered everything.

"Such a silky coat," said Mrs. Bensky, patting Benny's shiny head.

"For some strange reason, I was out of Vita-Grow this morning," Mr. Bensky complained, his mouth full of bacon and egg sandwich. "I had to use Wacky Watermelon. And now I smell like a girl!"

Rosie laughed. "You smell nice, Daddy," she said, smelling her father's hair. "Oops," she added, dropping a nice big piece of bacon to the floor for Benny.

"I know we can't hope for much in terms of dog obedience classes," Mr. Bensky said. "Let's face it, This dog is no Einstein. But I was thinking we could hope for a little *obedience*. We can hope for that, can't we?" he asked his wife. "A little obedience from this dog would sit fine with me." And he looked morosely down at Benny.

"Oh, yes. I'm sure we can hope for that," Mrs. Bensky said. "That's the whole idea behind obedience school."

Benny's eyebrows took on a worried line when he heard this word, 'obedience.' What a gloomy sounding word it was. Still, he was brave when Rosie snapped on his leash, kissed her parents good-bye, and left at a quarter to nine to walk Benny to the community center where the obedience classes were held.

"On your way?" Mr. Gormley from next door inquired a bit more cheerfully. "Not a moment too soon!"

"*Bonne chance!*" Molly the Mail Carrier called, giving them a thumbs up sign.

Benny didn't try to chase the first cat they saw, or the second one either. He didn't try to roll in flower beds or clamber up rock gardens. He simply walked along, putting one foot in front of the other.

"You're a good dog, Benny," Rosie told him quietly as they walked. "You're a brave dog. You're the hand-somest dog on the block."

When they reached the red-brick community center, Rosie went to the back door as her father had instructed.

The door was small, brown, and had no window. It had a sign, which had been fastened on with a solid row of nails across the top, bottom, and sides. "DOG OBEDIENCE CLASSES 9 A.M. SHARP," the sign read.

Rosie and Benny stared at the sign, but before Rosie had time to try the handle, someone opened the door slightly, snatched Benny's leash from Rosie's hands, and abruptly pulled Benny inside the door.

Up close, Ms. Viola Pin was tiny – hardly taller than Rosie – very thin and pointy looking. She was dressed entirely in black: a black leather miniskirt, black fishnet stockings, and black boots that were fringed around the top. Her eyes were green, sharp, and glittery. Her short red hair was spiked up like carpet tacks.

"Well, well. So it's the Perogy Palace pip-squeak," Ms. Viola Pin smirked, slapping a name tag onto Benny's chest. "How's your Daddy's business going?" she inquired, then laughed.

"I'm . . . I'm coming in with Benny," Rosie said quickly. But Benny could see the door already closing on Rosie's face.

"What does the sign say?" Ms. Viola Pin hissed through the narrowed doorway. "Speak up! What does it say?"

"It says, 'Dog Obedience Classes 9 A.M. sharp,'" Rosie answered.

"Are you a dog, then?" Ms. Viola Pin snapped. "Are you? Are you? Do you have four legs and a tail?"

"No," said Rosie.

"Then you're not allowed inside!" said the dog obedience teacher. "Be back at twelve sharp!" Then she slammed the door in Rosie's face and bolted it twice from the inside.

5

Stand! Sit! Stay! Heel!

Benny Bensky tried to look up at the dim, brown wall but was pulled quickly down a steep, cramped stairway. He glanced down once to admire his name tag but stumbled when his teacher jerked sharply on his leash.

At the bottom of the stairwell, Benny saw another windowless door with yet another sign nailed to it. His fiery-haired teacher unsnapped his leash, then pointed to a sign on the classroom door.

"Listen and remember," she said, reading the sign aloud in a crisp, icy voice:

CLASSROOM RULES

1. ATTENTION: COMPLETE ATTENTION!
2. CORRECTION: IMMEDIATE CORRECTION!
3. PERFECTION: ABSOLUTE PERFECTION!

"IS THIS UNDERSTOOD?" she barked.

Benny stared at the rules, then blinked rapidly.

Ms. Viola Pin opened the door, and they entered a large, low-ceilinged room lit here and there by hanging lightbulbs. There were several dozen dogs in the room, some of whom Benny thought he'd seen before. There was the little yellow dog he'd seen walking nicely on his leash. There was the large spotted one whose owner always pulled him away when Benny approached. And there was the large white dog who was never allowed off his front steps. Benny grinned in their direction, but they appeared not to notice him. Each dog was sitting in a small chalked-off square on the concrete floor, and each one was facing the front. All the dogs were completely silent.

"Quickly! Quickly!" Ms. Viola Pin shouted, indicating a tiny vacant square in the middle of a side row. Benny moved to the square as quickly as possible. "Tail *inside* the square!" she yelled, and Benny curled his tail around himself, trying to take up as little space as possible. "Spine straight!" she barked, and Benny did his best to straighten his back without moving his tail. "Now!" she commanded. "Eyes to the front!"

Benny looked toward the front, trying hard to remember the advice Rosie and Fran had given him. *Eyes to the front*, he told himself. *Stand up, sit down, raise your paw.* And in his eagerness to do well, he looked straight ahead, stood up, sat down, and raised his paw.

"Benny Bensky!" Ms. Viola Pin shrieked. "You are to remain MOTIONLESS until told to move! DO YOU UNDERSTAND?"

Benny replied by staring straight ahead. He remained as still as a lawn ornament. At the front of the room he saw a flip chart, a teacher's desk, and a clock. Benny could not believe his eyes. He felt ready to go home, but it was only three minutes after nine!

The walls were concrete, and the window – at least it looked to Benny like it might have once been a window – was boarded over from the inside.

"Daily drill!" Ms. Viola Pin barked. She began to call out commands in rapid succession: "Sit! Stand! Lie Down! Roll Over! Beg! Sit! Stand! Lie Down! Roll Over! Beg! Sit! Stand! Lie Down! Roll Over! Beg!"

Moving in perfect unison, all the dogs did exactly as their teacher commanded. But when Benny tried to follow, he was always a little – or sometimes more than a little – behind. When the others were standing, he was still sitting. When the others were rolling over, he was still scrambling to a stand. When the others were begging, he might still be lying down or rolling over.

"What are the rules of this classroom, Benny Bensky?" Ms. Viola Pin shouted. "Allow me to refresh your memory! One, attention, *complete attention*! Two, correction, *immediate correction*! Three, perfection, *absolute perfection!*"

Benny leaned forward, open-mouthed, listening so carefully, so intently, so painstakingly, that – suddenly – he hiccupped.

"Benny Bensky!" screamed Ms. Viola Pin. "I can see you are a troublemaker! Benny Bensky, to the front! Benny Bensky, you will see me after class for extra commands!"

Benny walked to the front and sat in the square chalked out beside his teacher's desk. He had a lump in his throat, and his brains felt like mush. The hands on the clock seemed hardly to move at all. Then he understood why. The hands on the clock were too scared to move!

"At-ten-*tion!*" the teacher screamed, and Benny jumped quickly to his feet and stood rigidly at attention, his back bristling with fear. Ms. Viola Pin turned to the flip chart where she had listed the names of all the dogs, Benny's near the bottom. Beside each name were rows of *x*'s and √'s.

"Today's lesson is *Heel!*" Ms. Viola Pin yelled, turning quickly to the class. "Heel!" she barked at Benny. "Heel! Benny Bensky, don't stand there! Heel!" Setting off at a brisk clip across the front of the room, she dragged him by his collar along with her.

Things seem to be getting off to a very poor start, Benny thought as he stumbled along as best he could behind her. *Things seem to be getting off on the wrong foot altogether.*

"Heel!" Ms. Viola Pin continued to shriek. "At my left! No cringing! Cringing is tomorrow's lesson! I said *HEEL!*"

At last Benny made it across the front of the classroom to the flip chart where he saw three rows of *x*'s already beside his name. The room was completely silent as Ms. Viola Pin's black felt-tipped marker squeaked and creaked across the flip chart.

From where Benny was standing, he could see the thinnest crack of sunshine from beneath the boarded

up window. So it really *was* a window! Outside that window, there would be grass, he told himself, maybe a few plump flies, maybe a nice smelly piece of garbage! How he wished he were in the park with Rosie and Fran right now!

Maybe this is just a bad dream, Benny told himself. *Maybe I am not really in dog obedience school at all. Maybe I am really frolicking in the tall grass in the leafy park.*

Suddenly the park seemed very real to Benny. *Rosie and Fran are playing on the swings nearby,* he thought. *The wind caresses my ears, the sun warms my shoulders. Smell the wildness of the river! Ahhh! Smell the cheese and crackers from Rosie and Fran's backpacks! Yummm! And look! Here comes my favorite truck, the Clean-All garbage truck that empties all the garbage bins in the park! What a rich aroma it has! What a lovely munching sound it makes! See its huge black tires! How rubbery they are! How plump! How inviting!*

And seeing his teacher's black leather skirt in front of him, imagining the pleasures of summer in the park, Benny Bensky dreamily lifted his leg and peed against Ms. Viola Pin's black miniskirt, down her black fishnet stockings, and into her fringed boots.

The classroom, already silent, suddenly took on an extra depth of silence. No one even breathed.

Benny roused himself from his daydream and gasped aloud. What – *oh what!* – had he done?

Ms. Viola Pin whirled around to flash her green eyes at him, then back to the flip chart where she wrote a big black *F* beside his name.

F is for Fail, Benny Bensky," she shrieked. She bent down and ripped off his name tag that read

HELLO, MY NAME IS BENNY, held it over the garbage can, and while Benny watched, ripped it into a hundred pieces.

"I have some new commands for you, Benny Bensky!" she said with a hard laugh. "Let's see if you can master these! Get lost! Vamoose! Scram! Beat it! Buzz off! Go home, you miserable mutt!"

With a hard clatter of boots on the floor, she led him out the door into the stairwell, to a smaller door under the stairs. She opened this small door, shoved Benny roughly inside, then slammed the door hard behind him.

6

Alone, Alone, All Alooooone!

Benny waited in the tiny dark room, unable, for a time, to see anything at all. There was no light, except for the faint light outlining the door. Slowly, however, his eyes began to make out other shapes in the room – a small shaggy shape and a larger, stout, rounded shape.

What had these dogs done? Benny wondered. They must have done something very bad to be here with him, though he hoped they had not done any-thing *quite* so unforgivable as he had! He waited politely for either one to speak, but neither looked in his direction nor moved at all.

Finally Benny wagged his tail and sniffed the small shaggy dog in a friendly doggy way. His nose encountered cold, damp strands of cotton. Why, it wasn't a dog at all. It was an old wet mop.

More cautiously now, Benny sniffed the stout dog. His nose bumped against rusted metal. This was no dog either. This was a grimy old wash bucket. Benny Bensky was locked in a closet with a mop and a bucket!

Benny threw himself on the concrete floor between the mop and the bucket. Presently, a little song came to his head, and he hummed it through, then sang it sadly to himself.

> *Alone, alone, all alooooone!*
> *Where, oh where, is my hooooome?*
> *I'm tired of school,*
> *I'm stuffed full of rules,*
> *And this floor is cold as a stooooone!*

What a fine song! thought Benny. *And my voice isn't bad either. I might not have much of a knack for obedience, but I do have a passable singing voice.* And, again, Benny sang:

> *Sometimes at home, I play and I roooooam,*
> *I sniff and I chase and I baaaaark,*
> *I eat a nice treat,*
> *(Maybe sa-la-mi!)*
> *And often I chew on a booooone.*

Benny sang the song several times, with feeling. Suddenly the door burst open and the broom closet was flooded with harsh artificial light.

"Benny Bensky! Who gave you permission to howl?" screamed Ms. Viola Pin, who crouched in the open doorway. "There will be no howling unless you are told to howl!"

Benny felt a leash being snapped onto his collar. He felt himself being jerked up the winding stairs, then shoved unceremoniously out the upstairs door into the blinding light of midday. His eyes were dazzled by the brightness, but not too dazzled to see that Rosie and Fran were there waiting for him.

Ms. Viola Pin handed Benny's leash to Rosie, then his report card with its row of angry black *F*'s down the entire page.

"Failed! Finished! Expelled!" Ms. Viola Pin announced triumphantly.

"Pardon?" Rosie said. Her face was still alight from her happiness at being reunited with Benny.

"He is a completely defective dog," Ms. Viola Pin gloated.

"Our Benny?" exclaimed Fran, hugging Benny. "Defective? Not our Benny!"

"He's disobedient, uncooperative, unruly, and antisocial," continued Viola Pin. "Unsuitable in every way." And she watched with cold satisfaction while Rosie and Fran read down the page of *F*'s.

"I hope your Daddy's precious Perogy Palace is more successful than his dog is," Ms. Viola Pin continued, staring hard at Rosie. "Location, location, location. A heritage building and those nice big picture windows. Your Daddy thinks he has it all, doesn't he? While a noteworthy educator like myself is forced to run my business from a dingy crowded basement. Tell me! Tell me! Does that seem fair to you?"

Rosie and Fran, with Benny between them, only looked at her, then took several steps backwards. But Ms. Viola Pin scurried close again and bent forward to focus in tight on Rosie. "You need to serve *good food* to make a restaurant a success, don't you?" She folded her bony arms and hunched forward looking at Rosie again. She smiled meanly. "How is your daddy doing in the *good food* department?"

7

A Totally Reformed Dog

Oh, the shame of it, thought Benny, as he lay on the floor of the tree fort, his head between his paws, his eyes scrunched shut. He remembered the hush that fell over the classroom when he did the awful thing that he'd done. He remembered how bare his chest felt without his new name tag. He remembered the loneliness of the dark broom closet, the look on Rosie and Fran's faces when they saw the row of *F*'s on his report card. He remembered the neighbors calling out, "Got the hang of obedience yet, Benny?" or, "Get sent to the principal's office yet, Benny? Ha, ha, ha!"

Rosie and Fran sat cross-legged on either side of Benny in the tree fort.

"Want to work on our Christmas lists, Rosie?" asked Fran. They kept a catalog in the tree fort for working on their Christmas lists, which they began in July.

"I don't feel like Christmas lists," Rosie answered.

"What about secret codes? We could make some new secret flashlight signals."

Usually Benny loved to hear the girls inventing new flashlight signals to send from the tree fort to Fran's house, which bordered the park. If Rosie and Benny got to the tree fort before Fran, they could signal her. They could, for example, send three long flashes (Come! Come! Come!) in the direction of Fran's bedroom window. And it was possible for Fran, who kept a flashlight on her window sill, to answer in three quick flashes (Yes! Yes! Yes!). But this time, neither Fran nor Rosie reached for the code book. No one spoke for a few minutes.

Finally Rosie looked at Benny, then Fran. "Let's promise to be friends forever," she said suddenly.

Fran shifted over so she could take Rosie's hand and Benny's paw. Rosie took Benny's other paw to complete the circle.

"Friends forever," Fran promised, squeezing firmly for emphasis.

"Friends forever," Rosie answered, squeezing back.

Friends forever! agreed Benny, thumping his tail on the plywood floor. *Yes, definitely! Friends forever!*

"I want to phone my mum and dad," Rosie said. "I want to tell them about obedience school."

"Come on, Benny," said Fran.

The three friends walked to the wading pool, where the lifeguard said that they could use the phone inside the swim shack.

"Hello?" Rosie said, her voice quavery. "Is this the Perogy Palace? Could I speak to my mum or dad, please?"

Rosie, Fran, and Benny huddled together inside the gloomy swim shack. Outside, the air was filled with bright sunshine, happy shrieks, and splashing water.

Rosie turned urgently to Fran. "You talk, Fran. You tell them!"

Fran took the phone. "Hello? Mr. Bensky? This is Fran. Yes, Rosie and I are fine but we thought we should tell you right now that Benny's obedience class didn't go exactly well. In fact, I would say it didn't go well at all. Actually, what I mean to say is, it went . . . well, . . . poorly."

As Fran spoke, Benny could feel water slowly dripping on his head from an overhead pipe but he was too sad to shake the water off, too miserable to move away from the drip.

"It went extremely poorly," Benny heard Fran explaining. "To tell the truth, Mr. Bensky, Benny got expelled."

"Expelled??!!" Benny could hear Mr. Bensky's voice on the line. He was yelling so loudly that Fran had to hold the phone away from her ear. "What? What? Expelled? That dumb mutt got expelled from obedience school? How can I hold my head up in this town? What now? What next?"

"Well, we told him," said Fran finally, when they'd hung up the phone and were walking sadly back home from the park.

"Yes," agreed Rosie. "We did."

Benny's feet felt as heavy as his heart, but he tried not to dawdle. He knew he'd caused enough trouble for one day.

From now on, Benny told himself, *I will be a totally reformed dog. From now on, I won't dig the dirt out of the plants or jump up on the couch the minute no one is looking. I won't chew the corners off the cushions, even though they do look cozier that way. From now on, I won't lick the butter when Rosie leaves it on the edge of the table. From now on, I won't throw myself against the door when the mailman comes or bite the mail when it comes through the slot. From now on,* Benny told himself firmly, *if anyone tells me to eat a perogy, I'll eat it. Definitely.*

Benny's resolutions cheered him considerably. As he walked obediently behind Rosie and Fran, he felt older and wiser. *Life is not a bowl of cherry-flavored doggie treats. I have to remember that,* he told himself sternly.

I will never again eat food from the sidewalk, he resolved.

Just then, Benny noticed some french fries on the path in front of him, but he looked away resolutely. He gave them a quick sideways look as he passed but looked away again. Then he found himself pulling back to sniff them.

I will never eat food from the sidewalk, he quickly decided, as he gulped them down. *Not unless it is a helping of perfectly fresh french fries or a heads-down ice cream,* he added, slurping down a strawberry cone a

little farther down the path. *Or, say, soft and chewy bubble gum, nicely melted on the sidewalk*, he told himself, coming upon a wad of sticky pink bubble gum.

And cats? he asked himself, as he spotted Ms. Viola Pin's white cat, Hairball, slinking along Ms. Viola Pin's back fence. *What is my rule for cats? Why, my rule for cats*, he decided, jerking the leash from Rosie's hands and launching himself, like a missile, after Hairball, *is I will never chase cats, except for Hairball, and except for this once.*

Benny's black furry body slammed hard against Ms. Viola Pin's fence, then catapulted after Hairball, who tore through the hedge, clawed up a drainpipe, and teetered to the top of the porch roof.

Roof! Roof! Benny barked. *Roof! Roof!*

Hairball glared down with cold green eyes.

Benny sat down on the ground beside the drainpipe and laughed. *What a joke*, he barked. *What fun! Come on, Hairball, let's do it again!*

8

A Tasty Supper

What a tasty supper that was," said Mrs. Bensky, as she cleared the table. "The dessert in particular. You're a good cook like your dad, Rosie." Rosie beamed, for she had made a cake herself from her favorite recipe:

Great Cake That's Fun to Make
1. Put these ingredients into a round baking pan:
   1½ cups flour
   1 cup sugar
   1 pinch salt

    1 teaspoon baking soda

    3 tablespoons cocoa powder

2. Mix.

3. Make 3 wells.

    Put 6 tablespoons oil in the first well.

    Put 1 tablespoon vinegar in the second well.

    Put 1 teaspoon vanilla in the third well.

4. Pour one cup water on top.

5. Mix.

6. Bake in 350° oven for 30 minutes.

Rosie had also decorated the cake to look like Benny, using two Cheerios for eyes, two orange jelly beans for eyebrows, an Oreo cookie for the nose, a piece of licorice for the mouth, and a strip of fruit leather cut in half for ears.

"She's a great cook like I used to be," Rosie's father said glumly. He stuffed the Oreo cookie into his mouth and covered the remainder of the cake with plastic wrap. "I used to be a first-rate perogy maker, but I've lost my touch. I'm all washed up now."

"You are *not* washed up," said Mrs. Bensky. "Your touch will come back. You'll be a first-rate perogy maker again."

"Yes, you will, Daddy," said Rosie, giving him a hug across his broad middle.

Even Benny, who was licking dirty plates in the open dishwasher, looked up and banged his tail sympathetically against the cupboard door.

"I put the flour and water and egg into the dough-making machine, just like I used to," Mr. Bensky said sadly. He slumped down on one of the kitchen chairs and his family gathered around him, Mrs. Bensky leaning back against the fridge, Rosie on another chair, Benny flopped at her feet.

"I put the dough into the roller," Mr. Bensky continued. "It rolls out the little balls of dough, the way it's supposed to, then the perogy filler stuffs them with different fillings, the same as always. The crimper crimps them, then I boil them. Everything totally normal. But what happens? They come out funny-tasting! They don't look too bad – a little gray, maybe – but they *are* bad! They taste just terrible!"

No one said anything. Even Benny looked dumbfounded by this.

"Pretty soon I'm going to be a good-for-nothing, like this dog here," Mr. Bensky said.

"He's *not* a good-for-nothing, Daddy!" Rosie said, covering Benny's floppy ears. "Don't say that. You'll hurt his feelings."

"I'd be surprised if he knew his own name."

"He *does* know his name," Rosie insisted. "He *does*."

"I'll bet he'd come no matter what you called him. I bet he comes if you call him *Twinkletoes!*"

"Let's try it," said Mrs. Bensky. "Here Twinkletoes, Twinkletoes. Here, Twinkletoes!"

Benny stayed where he was at Rosie's feet, though his eyebrows ping-ponged in puzzlement.

"You do it," Mr. Bensky said to Rosie. "He comes for your voice."

Rosie moved to the other end of the kitchen. "Here, Refrigerator!" she called. "Here, Refrigerator, Refrigerator, Refrigerator!"

But Benny only watched and listened.

"Here, Benny," said Mrs. Bensky, and Benny, wagging his tail, went to her immediately.

"Well, I'm surprised," said Mr. Bensky. "So he knows one thing. Pardon me, he knows *two* things. Number one, he knows where his dog dish is. Number two – forgive me for doubting it – yes, he does know his own name."

"He knows a lot of things," said Rosie. "He knows how to heel."

"He knows how to heel?" echoed Mr. Bensky. "Not according to his report card, he doesn't!" Mr. Bensky picked Benny's report card from the kitchen table and jabbed his finger at the angry black *F* beside the word 'Heel.'

"If I run fast enough, he does it," Rosie explained.

Rosie's parents laughed, and Benny stood up, grinning and wagging his tail to join in the joke, as he always did when he heard laughter.

"Exactly my point!" said Mr. Bensky. He picked up a dish towel and threw it over Benny's head. Benny froze, the dish towel over his head like a dust-cloth on a piece of furniture.

"See?" said Mr. Bensky. "Look at him! He's dazed, trapped, confused. He doesn't know which end is up. Face it. This dog is du–" Mr. Bensky stopped himself, cupped his hand around his mouth and whispered, "not that bright."

"He's being loyal, Daddy," said Rosie, looking down at Benny, who still had the dish towel draped over his head.

"Maybe he's just patient, dear," said Mrs. Bensky.

"Let's try it on you, Daddy," said Rosie, taking the dish towel off Benny's head and draping it over her father's. Mr. Bensky sat very still, the dish towel over his head as it had been over Benny's.

"I like it in here," he said finally. "I'm going to stay here."

Mrs. Bensky and Rosie laughed, and Benny joined in with a wag of his tail and a grin.

9

Every Dog a Perfect Dog, or Else!

Mrs. Bensky was filling the teapot when there was a sharp *ratta-tat-tat* at the front door.

"Ms. Viola Pin!" Benny heard Mrs. Bensky exclaim when she answered the door. "How . . . *interesting* . . . of you to drop by!"

Rosie poked her head from around the corner of the dining room, where she and her father were playing Crazy Eights.

"May I come in?" asked Ms. Viola Pin. Her green eyes glittered like Hairball's. Her hair was freshly gelled and standing in spikes on her head.

"Yes, of course," said Rosie's mother. "I've just made some raspberry tea."

"I have no time for tea," said Ms. Viola Pin, sitting down on the edge of the big blue chair in the living room. "I'm afraid this is not a social visit." Her furtive smile, however, gave her a look that was more pleased than afraid.

Rosie's parents sat down on the couch across from Ms. Viola Pin, with Rosie between them. Benny squeezed under the coffee table in the middle of the room.

It alarmed Benny to see his fiery-haired dog obedience teacher in his own front room, but he was curious too. Why had she come? What would she say? Had she maybe – by way of apology – brought a doggie treat? And if so, what type would it be? Doggie Doughnuts? Canine Crunch? Or his absolute favorite – mailman-shaped doggie biscuits?

Benny sniffed the air with his eraser-like nose and snapped at a housefly that had followed him under the table.

"To tell the truth," said Mr. Bensky, shaking his head, "I'm pretty unhappy about it too. My own dog getting expelled from dog obedience school! That isn't something I'm proud of."

Ms. Viola Pin cleared her throat in a businesslike way. "There is that unfortunate matter, yes. I found your dog, Benny Bensky, to be rude, disobedient, disruptive, inattentive, and in possession of a deeply ingrained antisocial attitude. You own a difficult and disturbed dog, which, I need not remind you, is a dangerous situation."

All four Benskys – Rosie, her mother and father, and Benny from beneath the coffee table – stared at Ms. Viola Pin, trying to absorb this information.

"However," Ms. Viola Pin said, "I have come about a second and more urgent matter, which again involves your dog, Benny Bensky." Here her glittery eyes gazed down at Benny, and Benny pulled his head and legs under the table like a turtle pulling into its shell.

On the other hand, thought Benny, *maybe she did not bring me a doggie treat.*

"Your dog, Benny," continued Ms. Viola Pin, "chased my rare and costly cat, Hairball, along my fence, through my hedge, up my drainpipe, and onto my porch roof."

"Ben-*ny*," said Mrs. Bensky reproachfully, and Benny pulled his tail under the coffee table too.

"Unlike your Benny," said Ms. Viola Pin, "my Hairball is of a naturally refined and delicate disposition. She suffers a paralyzing fear of heights, a tendency to heatstroke, and a predisposition to nightmares."

"Whoa-there!" said Mr. Bensky. "You just lost me."

"Hairball was trapped on the hot porch roof for two hours," elaborated Ms. Viola Pin, "and she would not come down until I enticed her with a full array of her favorite dishes – frog pie, mouse mousse, and bat brownies."

All four Benskys listened, open-mouthed. The fly circled Benny's head, and once more he brushed it away.

"Well, I certainly do apologize," said Mrs. Bensky.

Ms. Viola Pin waved her hand to indicate she had not finished speaking. "My lawyer urged me to take immediate action by reporting your dog to the police and having him declared a public nuisance. However, I am a fair and reasonable woman and I have come prepared to propose an alternative course of action."

Ms. Viola Pin paused, then took some papers from her black handbag and tapped them together. Underneath the coffee table, Benny felt dizzy and a little sick, as though he'd been twirling too long on the tire-swing at the park. He shook the fly from his left front paw, from his nose, from his back right paw. He tried to follow what was happening.

"I am prepared," said Ms. Viola Pin, "to give your dog another chance if you enroll him in my special program, *Extra Awful Dog Obedience Lessons*. As you can see from my brochure, my motto is, 'Every Dog a Perfect Dog, or Else.'

"Shortly we will be moving to a very convenient and spacious downtown location," she smirked, "which necessitates the rather steep rise in fees."

"Downtown location? That a fact?" said Mr. Bensky. "Where exactly will you be moving then?"

"I'm not at liberty to disclose that yet, I'm afraid."

Benny shook the fly off one ear, then off the other. He watched while the fly walked across the polished wood floor, up Ms. Viola Pin's black boot.

"Sign on the dotted line," smiled Ms. Viola Pin, standing to extend the form with one hand, a pen in the other. "This special offer is valid for only a brief time." She checked her watch. "In fact, this special offer expires at 8:00 this evening."

"But it's already five to eight!" said Mrs. Bensky.

"Could you run over the terms of this agreement again?" said Mr. Bensky, scratching his ear.

"Zzzzzzzzz," the fly taunted, flashing its blue wings at Benny. It was at the top of Ms. Viola Pin's black fringed boot now. "Zzzzzzzzzz!"

Benny lunged full force at the fly, his fangs bared. Ms. Viola Pin threw her hands in the air as Benny dove after the fly, to her left, to her right, then up behind her ear with ferocious speed, his white teeth snapping.

Ms. Viola Pin spun on her pointy black boots, then – screaming – collapsed backwards into her chair.

"Mad dog!" she screamed. "Help! Police! Mad dog!"

"Benny!" Mr. and Mrs. Bensky said together. But Benny was already on his back on the floor, his feet up in apology.

Stand straight! Face the front! Raise your paw! Stand for O Canada!*! Follow in single file! Don't cringe! Don't howl! Heel!* he told himself.

"Mad dog!" screamed Ms. Viola Pin again, jumping up onto the seat of her chair. "He bit me! He sank his teeth into me!"

"He was snapping at a fly!" said Rosie. "I saw him! He was only snapping at a fly!"

"He bit my arm! I mean, my ear! No, he bit my ankle!"

"Let me get you a cold drink," said Mrs. Bensky. "Let me get you an aspirin."

"Fools! Can't you see it's too late?" screamed Ms. Viola Pin. "You'll be sorry now!"

She pulled a black phone from her black purse and, without taking her eyes off Benny who still cowered on the floor, she tapped in a number.

Benny turned his eyes away, unable to meet her gaze. *Stand? Sit? Stay? Heel?*

"Hello? Police? This is Ms. Viola Pin, the acclaimed dog obedience teacher. I am calling to report a vicious dog. Come and remove him immediately. The dog is big, black, and extremely dangerous. His name is Benny Bensky."

An Awful Shame

The raspberry tea was well steeped by the time the police officers arrived, so the police officers set their police officer caps on the coffee table and drank a cup of tea with the Benskys.

"Not a bad dog, from what I see," Police Officer Sam said, making notes on a pad of paper.

"Reminds me of a pooch we had back home on the farm," Police Officer Sue said. And Police Officer Sam wrote that down too.

"Benny didn't bite his teacher," Rosie said, bravely speaking up. "He was just catching a fly."

"Where is that darned fly anyway?" asked Mr. Bensky, looking up at the ceiling. "Did Benny get him?"

"Benny forgot his manners," explained Rosie's mother.

"He's got a brain the size of a pea, but he's not mean," said Rosie's father.

Benny watched with interest while Police Officer Sam wrote this down as well, illustrating it with a circle the size of a pea.

"It's an awful shame," Police Officer Sue said, putting her empty cup on the coffee table.

"What do you mean?" Rosie's mother asked quickly. "You're not saying there's a problem, are you? Everything's okay, isn't it?"

"Do you know anyone on a farm who can take him?" Police Officer Sam asked. He put his pen behind his ear and his pad of paper in his shirt pocket.

"No!" Rosie said, throwing her arms around Benny's neck. "No! I'd never give him away!"

"The problem is," Police Officer Sue said, "now there is a Vicious Dog Report filed against him."

"We don't know anyone in the country who could take him," said Mr. Bensky, looking worried for the first time. "He fits just fine here in Smith Falls, as far as we're concerned."

"It's exactly because of sad situations like this that we recommend dog-owners take their dogs to dog obedience classes," Police Officer Sam said.

"Benny *did* go to dog obedience classes," Rosie said, then frowned. "I mean, he went to *one* dog obedience class."

"We have that information on file as well," said Police Officer Sue. "Just today his teacher filed a report on his uncooperative and antisocial behavior. I'm sorry."

"What does 'antisocial' mean?" asked Rosie, near tears now.

"Bad, bad, very bad. Big *B* bad. That's what 'antisocial' means," said Police Officer Sue.

Benny felt Police Officer Sue's words rain down like blows. He hung his head in shame.

The police officers put their police officer caps back on their heads, stood side by side, their feet apart, and spoke in unison.

"Inasmuch as a Vicious Dog Report has been filed against Benny Bensky, the aforesaid Benny Bensky is hereby and forthwith declared a Public Nuisance. And you, Benny Bensky, have twenty-four hours to get out of the town of Smith Falls."

11

Twenty-four Hours
to Get out of Town

*T*wenty-four hours to get out of Smith Falls! Benny thought. He lay beside Rosie, his head on her pillow, but his eyes wide open.

Was there an outside to Smith Falls? His home was in Smith Falls. Rosie was in Smith Falls. Fran was in Smith Falls. The park and the tree fort were in Smith Falls. So were Vito's Videos and the Perogy Palace. Every sewer grate and fire hydrant and back alley he knew were in Smith Falls. Even the perfect upside-down dish that was the sky, fit snugly over this town that he loved – Smith Falls. What could possibly be left over for the *outside* of Smith Falls?

From the kitchen, Benny could hear Mr. and Mrs. Bensky's voices.

"I'll put an ad on the bulletin board at the Perogy Palace," Mrs. Bensky said. "But twenty-four hours is not much time at all." She sighed. "Listen to this. This is what I have so far: 'Large black dog, excellent with children, needs out-of-town home immediately.'"

"Excellent with children, sure, but not much else," said Mr. Bensky. Then plaintively he added: "Who's going to baby-sit Rosie when we're at the Perogy Palace? If that mutt was good for nothing else, he was a good sitter."

"How will we know if he's going to a good home?" worried Mrs. Bensky. "You read such terrible things in the paper. I don't want him to end up as a junkyard dog. He's used to having a family. He's used to having a real home."

"I know."

"Okay, then," Mrs. Bensky said after a while. "Listen to this ad: 'Large black dog – excellent with children, likeable, loyal – needs out-of-town home immediately.'"

"He's got a sense of humor," said Mr. Bensky. "Put

that down too. A sense of humor's not a small thing. A sense of humor's in short supply in some quarters."

"I know what you mean," answered Mrs. Bensky, then read the ad aloud again: "'Large black dog – excellent with children, likeable, loyal, good sense of humor – needs out-of-town home immediately.'"

Listening from Rosie's bedroom, Benny wished this was all a dream. But no dream – or even nightmare – he'd ever had came close to this. He'd never dreamed that he had to leave Rosie. He'd never dreamed that he had to leave the place he called home. He'd never dreamed of Mr. and Mrs. Bensky sitting in the kitchen writing an advertisement to find some other home for him.

In addition to this, Benny had never dreamed – or even daydreamed – that he overheard a compliment from Mr. Bensky!

Benny felt Rosie wrap her arms around his tense shoulders. "Don't worry, Benny," she whispered into his ear. "We'll run away together. There are places in the country. There are haystacks. There are barns. There has to be some place we can go. We'll find it, Benny. We will." Benny felt her hug him even tighter. "I'll never let them take you away from me, Benny. Never."

Benny licked Rosie's face and jumped to the floor, jingling his collar. *Maybe there is a way to make everything work out,* he thought.

"Not yet," Rosie cautioned. She stroked his muzzle. "We have to wait until everyone's asleep."

Through Rosie's screened bedroom window, Benny could hear a chorus of frogs from the river, the distant sound of traffic on the other side. From somewhere else, there was the howl of a lonely dog. But finally their own house was still. The only sound was Mr. Bensky's steady snoring from the other bedroom.

"Shhh," Rosie whispered. Benny tried hard to remember not to thump his tail against the bedroom door. Rosie dressed in shorts and a T-shirt, with a sweatshirt on top for warmth in the cool night air.

"I wish Fran was here," Rosie said aloud. She looked at the kitchen clock. "But it's after ten. It's too late to call her."

Rosie tiptoed to the front closet for her backpack, unzipped it and put in a box of juice, a package of soda crackers and a handful of dog biscuits. She opened the fridge and took several cheese-sticks. Then, by the light of the open refrigerator, she wrote a note for her parents.

Dear Mum and Dad,
I love you now and I love you forever.
*   From your daughter,*
*   Rosie. xoxoxoxoxoxo*
*   P.S. Benny loves you too.*

She attached the note to the clothespin magnet on the fridge door. Rosie's dad stopped snoring for a moment. Rosie and Benny looked at each other. Then Mr. Bensky began snoring even louder than before.

Rosie quietly opened the side door, and Benny followed her out.

In the darkness, there was the smell of cut grass, the soft swish of sprinklers. Rosie looked one way down the night street, then the other. She and Benny moved closer to each other.

"Let's go to the tree fort first, Benny," Rosie said at last.

Reflections of the streetlights shone in the river and the bullfrogs bragged to one another. Above them, the stars of the Big Dipper twinkled. But Benny only hunched his furry shoulders and followed Rosie, close enough that he could touch her leg with his nose from time to time as they walked.

If only I hadn't snapped at that fly, he thought. *If only I hadn't chased Hairball. If only I hadn't thought of the black tires of the Clean-All garbage truck when my teacher was writing on the flipchart. If only I had eaten that perogy. If only I were a nicer, better, and more perfect dog. If only – if only! – I were some other dog altogether!*

Yikes!

The bark of the willow tree was rough and cool in the darkness, the leaves black and whispery. Rosie guided Benny up the slanting trunk into their tree fort, then climbed up herself.

Benny nosed around to find the flashlight, then dropped it into Rosie's lap.

"It's too late, Benny," Rosie said. "Fran will be asleep by now."

But Benny nudged the flashlight again.

Rosie pointed the flashlight in the direction of Fran's house and sent three long flashes (Come!

Come! Come!). She sent the signals again and again.

"My finger's tired, Benny," Rosie said at last. Her voice sounded very small in the blackness. "I'm tired too. What are we going to do, Benny?"

From a house near the park there was the sound of a guitar, laughing, and singing. "There ain't no flies on us!" someone sang. "No, there ain't no flies on us!"

The plywood floor of the tree fort – so comfortable in the daytime – seemed damp and cold and hard at night. Benny leaned against Rosie in the darkness.

Suddenly, from Fran's house, there were three short bursts of colored lights (Yes! Yes! Yes!). The entire string of colored patio lights behind Fran's house flashed quickly in secret code. (Yes! Yes! Yes!)

"She sees it!" cried Rosie, hugging Benny in the darkness. "She sees it, Benny!"

"I know all about it," Fran panted when she arrived minutes later. "I know what happened." She was talking so quickly her words tumbled over each other. "My mum and dad and I were returning a video, and Vito told us that he'd heard that Benny bit Ms. Viola Pin and that the police gave Benny twenty-four hours to leave Smith Falls!"

"But Benny *didn't* bite her!" Rosie protested. "*He didn't!*"

"I know," said Fran, who was catching her breath, her arms around Benny. "I knew Benny wouldn't do that. Would you, Benny? Vito didn't believe it either."

Benny licked Fran's face in the darkness, and Fran laughed.

"We went to the Perogy Palace, my mum and dad and me," Fran continued. "My mum and dad wanted to talk to your mum and dad. We could see your dad working in the kitchen in the back, but the door was locked and he couldn't hear us knocking."

Benny felt Rosie shake her curly head in the darkness.

"But my dad's not at the Perogy Palace. My dad's asleep in bed."

"But I just saw him there," said Fran.

"The Perogy Palace has been closed all evening," said Rosie.

No one spoke for a moment. Then Benny, who was listening carefully, growled.

"I saw your dad," and here Fran paused dramatically, "or I saw someone who *looked* like your dad."

"You mean . . .?" Rosie asked.

"Exactly. We better check this out, Rosie. Come on, Benny."

The three friends walked quickly down the night streets of Smith Falls toward the Perogy Palace. Benny kept his head down, hoping no one would ask why they were out so late, whether they needed help

getting home, or if he was the dog who had twenty-four hours to get out of town. They passed the bank machine, they passed Vito's Videos and continued. They didn't look left or right.

When they arrived at the Perogy Palace, they could see the blue neon sign was on, the lights inside were lit, but the slatted blinds were shut.

Rosie went up the wooden steps and peeked in along the edge of the blinds. She stared, speechless for a moment, at what she saw.

"Holy Smokes!" she said, finally. "Look at this, Fran." Fran took her turn looking in along the edge of the blinds.

"I can't believe this," Fran said, after several moments. "Or can I?"

Then Rosie and Fran hoisted Benny up to give him a look.

Yikes! Benny yelped and wiggled down. Benny took a step backwards, and the fur on the back of his neck bristled. What he'd seen inside the Perogy Palace made a low growl of fear come to his throat.

13

No Wonder the Perogies Taste Funny!

T he front door of the Perogy Palace is locked," Rosie said, shaking the door handle.

Whew! thought Benny. *That suits me!* He looked up at his friends and turned toward the sidewalk, jingling his collar expectantly. *Come on!* his eyes said. *Let's go!*

"Let's try the fire door," Rosie said, and led the way down the narrow passage beside the Perogy Palace to the back. Fran followed, then – more reluctantly – Benny.

At the back, they saw a line of light along three sides of the door. When they got closer, Benny saw the door was being held open by a broom handle.

"Come on," Fran said, pulling the door open, and tiptoeing inside.

Rosie followed. Benny hung back, whimpering a little. But he hesitated only for a moment. What he'd seen inside the Perogy Palace was terrible and frightening, but there was one thing that was even more terrible and frightening to Benny: the thought of being separated from his best friends.

Benny shuffled in through the door, his shoulders rounded, his head down, his tail curled between his legs, but his courage tucked tight inside him.

Inside the back entrance of the Perogy Palace, the three friends stood quietly in the shadows of the many bags of flour that were neatly stacked against the side wall. Together they stared in the direction of the figure at the far end of the Perogy Palace kitchen.

The figure was small, yet severe – not at all like Mr. Bensky from this distance. But she was dressed (for the figure did seem to be a girl, or a very small woman) in Mr. Bensky's cook's uniform. The white hat flopped down over her forehead, and the sleeves of the white jacket were rolled up. Below the jacket, Rosie, Fran, and Benny could see thin, fishnet-stockinged legs and fringed black boots.

The person in the Perogy Palace kitchen, wearing the Perogy Palace cook's uniform, was none other than Ms. Viola Pin.

Yikes! Benny said to himself again. *Double yikes!* He flattened his ears to his head and curled his tail even tighter.

As they watched, Ms. Viola Pin carried a step-ladder to one of the stainless steel machines, then dumped a brown paper bag of something into the hopper.

"That's the dough machine," Rosie whispered. "My dad puts flour and water and eggs in that machine, and little balls of dough come out, ready for rolling and stuffing."

"The question is," Fran whispered back, "*What* is she putting into the machine? And *why?*"

The threesome continued to watch. And while they watched, Ms. Viola Pin emptied a brown paper bag into every machine in the room – into the mixer, the roller, the filler, the crimper, even into the vats of fresh water ready for boiling the perogies the next day.

Rosie crept to the control panel with its many

buttons, lights, and levers. Benny carefully followed, then Fran. They crouched behind, Rosie watching from the top of the control panel, Fran from one side, and Benny – his eyebrows raised – from the other side.

There were hand-printed labels on the bags Ms. Viola Pin was emptying into the fillings Mr. Bensky had prepared earlier that day.

"What do the labels say?" Rosie whispered, squinting to read that distance.

"Walls-r-Us Wallpaper Paste," Fran read quietly aloud, "Klean-Kat Kitty Litter, Home-grown Mealy Worms, Soggy Sawdust."

Rosie, Fran, and Benny stared at each other.

"No wonder the perogies taste funny!" Rosie said, a little louder than she intended. "My poor dad!"

Ms. Viola Pin picked up the last brown bag and poured it into the strawberry filling, which was Rosie and Fran's favorite. "HOT AND HORRIBLE BLACK PEPPER – HA! HA! HA!," the label read.

"Ahhh . . .," Benny said aloud, shaking his head a little, his eyes watering, "Ahhhhh . . ."

"Don't sneeze, Benny!" Rosie begged. Rosie clamped her hands around Benny's muzzle, and Fran clamped her hands over his ears.

"Ahhh . . . AH-CHOOO!!" Benny barked aloud.

Rosie and Fran ducked behind the control panel just as Ms. Viola Pin whirled around.

"Oh, it's only *you*," Viola Pin sneered, when she saw Benny. "The mangy mutt who's got twenty-four hours to get out of town. Aren't you getting a little pressed for time? Or have you already found a watch-dog job

in some lonely locked garage?" She laughed aloud.

Benny stared at her and took several steps backwards.

"Well, never mind," she said. "If you don't come up with something soon, the police will take care of you."

She smiled, her green eyes glittering, then slowly began to walk toward him.

"Maybe you don't *know* what happens to little doggies the police officers take away," Ms. Viola Pin purred. "Maybe no one's had the heart to tell you. Well, let me be the one to fill you in with all the details."

Stealthily, Rosie and Fran moved in behind the crimper so they could watch Benny but, at the same time, remain hidden from Ms. Viola Pin.

"First of all," continued Ms. Viola Pin, "the police will take you to a lonely locked cell with nothing in it but a cold wet concrete floor. Sound nice?" Ms. Viola Pin smiled. "You're alone. All, all, alone. Think about it, Benny Bensky." She smiled again in a cozy way, as if she were his very best friend. "Remember being lost on the streets of Smith Falls without a friend in the world? Remember being locked into the broom closet? Well, this time . . ."

Benny heard her voice go on and on. He tried not to listen. He held his floppy ears tight to his head. But even this did not block out her persistent, penetrating voice and the terrible things she was saying.

"NO!" he heard Rosie say suddenly. Benny turned his head and was horrified to see that Rosie had jumped up from behind the crimper and was boldly facing Ms. Viola Pin. "NEVER! That will NEVER happen to Benny! NEVER!"

"NO ONE can say things like that to our dog!" Fran added, jumping up to stand on the other side of Benny. "NO ONE can talk to our Benny like that! NO ONE!"

14

How Could He Ever Explain?

Well, well, well. Isn't this a touching sight!" Ms. Viola Pin smirked, staring at the trio who stood before her. "You'll have to excuse me if I fail to shed a sentimental tear, but I've just mislaid my handkerchief!"

She folded her skinny arms, pulled her head back on her bony neck, narrowed her glittering green eyes, and stared calculatingly at them.

Benny's heart was pounding in his chest, his throat felt dry, his legs a trifle shaky. But with intrepid Rosie on his right and valiant Fran on his left, he felt more stouthearted and more daring than he would have on his own. Benny breathed as deeply as his broad chest allowed, squared his furry doggie shoulders, and looked directly into the eyes of his fearsome dog obedience teacher.

It was silent for a full minute. All of Benny's senses were completely alert. No one moved a finger, a toe, or a paw.

Abruptly, Ms. Viola Pin threw her hands helplessly in the air.

"Oh, dear! Oh, dear! Oh, dear!" she cried piteously. Her voice was high pitched and quavery. She covered her face with her pointed fingernails and shook her red spiked head to and fro, as if in abject remorse. "Well, I confess I'm quite defeated! I give up! I surrender! You three are far more clever than me!" And she hung her spiky head in a show of meekness.

Still bent into her remorseful stance, she paused and peeked between her fingers to check the reaction of the threesome.

"If only I could make this up to you!" she continued. Her voice was trembling and tearful.

Suddenly she brightened. "Oh, I know what I can do! I can help you save that pathetic, doomed, and wretched dog of yours — save him from the terrible

terrible trouble he's in. How I pity him. How I would love to help."

She opened the door to the large vegetable cooler at the back of the kitchen and, with a sweep of her hand, invited Benny, Fran, and Rosie to step in ahead of her. "Come in," she purred, pulling her mouth into a sympathetic smile. "Come in, friends, and we'll talk about what we can do to save your poor pathetic Benny."

"But we're not the only ones in trouble, Ms. Pin," Fran pointed out in her frank and logical way. "*You're* in trouble too. *You're* the one who came into Mr. Bensky's Perogy Palace, where you have no right to be!"

There was a sudden hiss, and a whirl of cold air as Ms. Viola Pin spun around in front of the open door of the vegetable cooler. She pointed at them with her bony finger.

"So this is your gratitude!" she hissed, her teeth almost as sharp and pointed as Hairball's. "Yet you – *you!* – have the dog who's been labelled a Public Nuisance! "You – *you!* – have the dog who's doomed to exile!" She glared at them with her dazzling and furious green eyes.

Benny felt faint, almost dizzy. What his dog obedience teacher said was true. He was surrounded by trouble at every side. Terrible trouble! Rosie and Fran seemed to wilt on either side of him too, as if they were momentarily thrown off balance as well.

For a moment, both Fran and Rosie seemed too downhearted to respond.

"But how do we know you'll help us?" Rosie finally said in a small, uncertain voice. "How do we know you're telling the truth?"

"Oh, but I *am*. I promise you, I *am*." Ms. Viola Pin purred, all smiles now. "In fact – Wait just a minute." She placed a finger thoughtfully on her scissory chin, then smiled at them with her glittering green eyes. "Why, this very moment I thought of the exact thing that would make Benny Bensky a free dog tomorrow. Tonight, in fact!"

Rosie and Fran looked at each other for a long moment then linked hands. "Come on, Benny," they said, stepping together toward the open door of the vegetable cooler.

But Benny hesitated.

"Come along, Benny," Ms. Viola Pin encouraged, her pointy teeth shining. She bent down to whisper to him in a confidential way. "You must be part of our secret plan too."

Ms. Viola Pin's words, a 'Public Nuisance,' 'Doomed to Exile,' hung like black flags in Benny's mind. But her other words, 'A Free Dog by Tomorrow,' and 'A Secret Plan,' hung like white flags in his mind right beside the black ones.

He looked into the shadowy cooler at the baskets of eggs, the bowls of strawberries, the boxes of mushrooms, the foil-wrapped cubes of butter – all the delicious foods neatly lined up on the shelves in front of him. He looked at the tubs of sour cream, at the bushel baskets of onions. He looked at Ms. Viola Pin, who stood beside the open door of the cooler – smiling glitteringly, nodding her head reassuringly – beckoning them with a crook of her pointy finger.

Instantly, and without taking time to reason things out – only *knowing* in his deep-down-doggie-way – Benny leapt into the doorway in front of Rosie and Fran, and barked sharply to warn them. Something was amiss! Something was not right!

No! No! Benny barked. *No! No! No!*

"It's a trick!" Fran shouted, "Don't go in, Rosie!"

Benny saw Rosie and Fran turn and start to run, calling over their shoulders for him to follow. But –

oh, no! – Benny saw Rosie trip on a lever connected to the control panel, and fall full length to the floor!

All the machines in the kitchen surged into motion. The mixer began mixing, the roller began rolling, the crimper began crimping, the perogy filler began squirting little dollops of filling into the air.

"Come back! Come back!" screamed Ms. Viola Pin, running after them. "Fools! Don't be afraid of me! I want to help you, remember?"

Abruptly, Benny came to a sideways standstill, causing Ms. Viola Pin to trip over his furry back and fall headlong to the floor.

"You mean, moth-eaten, miserable mongrel!" she screeched, shaking her fist at him. "You did that on purpose, didn't you? You double-crossing mutt! And look, you made me break the heel of my boot!"

She pulled off the boot with its broken heel, threw it at Benny, and lurched to a standing position. She was wearing only one boot now.

Ms. Viola Pin's tumble had given Fran and Rosie time to jump up and hide behind the large silvery mixer.

Now that Ms. Viola Pin's attention was fastened on him, Benny led her on a merry chase around the crimper, under the perogy filler, between the mixer and the roller, then round and round the crimper again. He bounced along easily, running just fast enough to keep her in furious, hobbling pursuit.

"You worthless fleabag!" she panted as she hobbled after him. "You miserable cur!"

From the corner of his eye, Benny saw Rosie and Fran scrambling up the bags of flour that were stacked against the far wall of the Perogy Palace kitchen. He spun easily on his heels and led Ms. Viola Pin in the opposite direction.

But when they crawled out from under the perogy filler and rounded the mixer for the forty-seventh time, Viola Pin twisted her head around and spotted Rosie and Fran, who were perched safely on top of the bags of flour.

"Ha, ha! So you thought you could get away from me!" she screeched, doubling back on them.

Benny's fur bristled on his back, a growl rose in his throat, and he bounded back after her – full speed this time.

Ms. Viola Pin was already scrambling up the bags after the girls, the heel of her one good boot as effective for climbing the steep wall of bags as a mountain climber's hob-nailed shoe. She turned around as she climbed and tipped one bag of flour from the pile on to Benny – then another one.

Benny dodged the first bag, then dodged the second one – though both bags split open on the floor, sending white clouds of flour into the air.

"Look at the mess you made!" the dog obedience teacher screeched triumphantly from high on top of the bags of flour. "You'll be sorry now!" Then she loosened a small avalanche of bags on top of Benny. One bag hit Benny squarely on the shoulders – knocking the wind out of him – another hit him on the back, while yet several others fell on top.

"Ha, ha, ha!" he heard someone laughing shrilly, "hee, hee, hee!"

Benny Bensky felt himself trapped in darkness under the heavy bags. He couldn't move. He couldn't even catch his breath! Where was he? Why was it still so dark?

Then, as if in a dream, Benny heard other voices. He heard Fran and Rosie's voices! They were calling him from what seemed a great distance away.

"Help!! Help!! Benny!! Benny!! Heeeelp!!"

Benny heard their calls, and summoned the truest, bravest, and most noble part of himself. He braced himself and pushed powerfully with his broad shoulders, kicked ferociously with his sturdy legs, resisted fiercely with his long wide back.

Then suddenly, with terrific canine force, he burst free from the crushing weight of the bags, into the light, and found himself flying through the air to the other side of the kitchen, where Rosie and Fran were being pushed into the vegetable cooler by Ms. Viola Pin.

"So! The Perogy Palace pip-squeaks need a little help getting into the cooler!" he heard Ms. Viola Pin laughing as he hurled himself against her with terrific force.

Benny would do anything – *everything* – to save his Rosie. Benny would do anything – *everything* – to save his Fran. He bared his powerful fangs, and a low and fearsome rumble came from deep inside his chest.

"Help, Police! Someone help!" cried Ms. Viola Pin as she tumbled to the floor. She cringed as she crawled backwards away from Benny. "Help!"

"Come on!" yelled Fran, as she and Rosie ran to the control panel. Rosie pressed the red button and a fire alarm went off. Fran pressed the blue button and a burglar alarm began to clang.

Benny's throat rumbled menacingly as he closed

the distance between himself and his dog obedience teacher. He could not let Ms. Viola Pin come near Rosie or Fran again!

"Nice doggie! Good doggie!" Ms. Viola Pin said, crawling gingerly backwards from him. Both she and Benny were still white with flour.

Relentlessly, Benny moved after her, vicious growling erupting from his throat. Ms. Viola Pin crawled backwards even faster across the floor of the Perogy Palace kitchen.

"Stay!" Ms. Viola Pin screeched, cowering before him. "Heel! Sit! Lie down!"

She crawled backwards past the mixer, past the crimper, past the roller, past the perogy filler. Still growling ferociously, Benny advanced – his head low, his fangs bared.

When Ms. Viola Pin bumped backwards against the sink, Benny seized her shirt with his powerful teeth, stood up on his sturdy back legs, and dropped his shrieking dog obedience teacher neatly into the sink.

Automatically, the sink began to fill with soap and water.

"Help! Help!" screamed Ms. Viola Pin, her arms and legs thrashing frantically. She was wedged, up to her armpits, in soapy water.

Suddenly, the doors of the Perogy Palace burst open, and Police Officers Sue and Sam ran in with their flashlights on high.

"What seems to be the problem here?" Police Officers Sue and Sam asked, shining their flashlights into Ms. Viola Pin's eyes.

"This dog attacked me!" screamed Ms. Viola Pin, still up to her armpits in sudsy water. "He tripped me! He doused me in flour! He threw heavy bags at me! He trapped me in this sink of water and, oh yes, he also bit me!"

Benny, who was still white with flour, looked worriedly at Police Officers Sue and Sam. Would they believe her? How could he ever explain? What would they think? What would happen now?

"And I thought I'd seen everything," said Police Officer Sam, shaking his head sadly.

"Who knows what evil lurks in the heart of man . . . er, dog," said Police Officer Sue.

"Yesterday, we booked a black dog, and today, a white one," said Police Officer Sam, taking his report pad from his breast pocket and licking the tip of his pencil.

"But she was trying to lock us into the vegetable cooler!" said Fran.

"And look what she poured into the machines!" said Rosie. "She's wrecking my dad's perogies! She's ruining my dad's restaurant!"

"I'll bet this is not the first time Ms. Viola Pin tampered with these machines!" said Fran.

Rosie and Fran pointed to the brown paper bags, which still lay scattered across the floor.

"See?" they said together. "Walls-r-Us Wallpaper Paste! Klean-Kat Kitty Litter! Home-grown Mealy Worms! Soggy Sawdust! Hot and Horrible Black Pepper – Ha! Ha! Ha!"

"Ahh-chooo!" sneezed Benny, remembering.

"If you check the handwriting on the labels, I suspect you'll find it matches the handwriting of Ms. Viola Pin," said Rosie.

"I suggest you dust for fingerprints before removing any of the evidence," added Fran.

"Don't believe them!" sputtered Ms. Viola Pin, splashing bubbles over the lip of the sink. "Let me go home! What do these pathetic Perogy Palace pipsqueaks know anyway?"

Police Officer Sue and Police Officer Sam surveyed the scene. Leaving Ms. Viola Pin where she was, they photographed the paper bags, dusted for fingerprints, and measured the exact distance between the paper bags, the machines, and Ms. Viola Pin. They placed all the paper bags in separate plastic envelopes and made notations in their notebooks.

"Fools!" screamed Ms. Viola Pin, splashing helplessly in the bubbles. "You ruined all my plans! Now there never will be a Deluxe Dog Obedience Academy here. Don't you see the priceless advantage of the prime downtown location? Of the spacious quarters? Of the large picture windows? Don't you see how perfect it would have been?" She glared at all of them, sloshing soapsuds over the lip of the sink. "Can't you just imagine it divided into classrooms, detention halls, drill areas and cages?? It isn't fair! It just isn't fair!

"I would have been world famous! I would have made every dog a perfect dog! Why, just look at that miserable specimen!" she spluttered, pointing at Benny. "He's got no form! He's got no style! First, I'd have chopped off his tail. Then I'd have put implants in his ears to make them stand up properly. Then, with all this lovely space, I could have branched into perfecting cats and parakeets!"

The kitchen of the Perogy Palace was absolutely silent as everyone absorbed the words of Ms. Viola Pin.

"Holy Cow!" Police Officer Sue said at last. She shook her head in disbelief. "This is a sad day for you, Ms. Viola Pin, but a happy day for the citizens of Smith Falls."

Police Officer Sam handcuffed Ms. Viola Pin, and Police Officer Sue led her, dripping, to the waiting police van.

"It wasn't my fault, Officer," Ms. Viola Pin whined as she left through the fire door of the Perogy Palace.

"That mangy mutt jiggled my arm and made me spill the bags into the machines!"

"I advise you to save your story for the judge, M'am," Police Officer Sue quietly replied.

"Look at this dog," Police Officer Sam said. "I could have sworn that a minute ago he was a white dog."

Benny scratched himself, and the flour flew off in puffs of white. He stuck out his tongue and licked his nose.

"Now his nose is black!" said Police Officer Sue.

Benny licked his paw, wiped his face, scratched himself again. Slowly, he became blacker and blacker.

Benny grinned up, and the Police Officers knelt down – their eyes wide with recognition – and grinned back.

15

Every Dog Has His Day

"Shake-a-paw!" Police Officer Sue said with a broad smile.

They were standing beneath the pink, blue, and yellow streamers that criss-crossed the ceiling of the Perogy Palace. Behind them, banners in the window read:

IN THE GROOVE AND ON THE MOVE!

BACK IN BUSINESS BASH!

Benny reached out his black paw to Officer Sue and they shook. Then he shook hands with Police Officer Sam.

The crowd of friends and neighbors inside the Perogy Palace applauded wildly. The red-haired reporter from *The Smith Falls Times* took notes. Lightbulbs flashed. The small yellow dog, the large spotted dog, and the large white dog Benny recognized from Ms. Viola Pin's Dog Obedience Class were there with their owners, and they barked their approval and wagged their tails.

The Mayor presented Benny with a Pardon. "Every dog has his day," the mayor said solemnly, "as someone once observed." The Mayor shook Benny's paw. The crowd stamped and cheered.

The Mayor then held up three gold medals with the word 'HERO' engraved on each one. He placed one around Benny's neck, another around Rosie's neck, and the third around Fran's neck.

"When one of our families is in trouble, we're all in trouble," the Mayor said. "When one of our families is pulled to safer ground, we're – all of us – pulled to safer ground."

Everyone clapped again. Billy Bittle the Barber threw his cap in the air, Molly the Mail Carrier yelled,

"Ya-hooo!" Vito did a little jig, and Mr. Bensky whistled between his fingers. Even grumpy Mr. Gormley had a huge smile.

"Now for the surprise part of this special ceremony," the Mayor said, and Police Officers Sue and Sam stepped forward.

Police Officer Sam pulled a thick sheaf of notes from his jacket pocket, cleared his throat, and began to read in a low, monotonous voice.

"In all tales of heroism, suspense, and adventure, I believe it is a good idea to start at the beginning. My name, as most of you know, is Sam. I was born at a very young age with a full head of handsome blond hair ..."

"Cut to the chase!" Mr. Bensky shouted, and the crowd chuckled.

Police Officer Sam grinned good naturedly, and put his notes down.

"This is as short as I can make it," he said, and held out a police hat with the name 'BENNY' embroidered in gold across it. "The Smith Falls Police Department wants to have you, Benny Bensky, as our ambassador – our symbol, if you like – of Good Will." Here he paused and looked directly at Benny. "Benny Bensky, will you be our Mascot?"

"Ben-*ny!*" the crowd chanted. "Ben-*ny!* Ben-*ny!*"

Then, gradually, the crowd grew silent. Everyone craned their necks to look at Benny. Everyone wondered what he would do.

Benny looked at the blue police hat with the shiny visor, the buttons at the sides, his name, 'BENNY,' in gold letters across the front.

Benny thought about being in the coffee shop eating doughnuts with Police Officer Sue and Police Officer Sam. "Do you prefer the peanut butter–iced doughnut, or the custard-filled cruller, Benny?" he imagined Police Officer Sue asking.

Then Benny found himself looking across the restaurant at Fran, who sat quietly in a row of chairs near the kitchen.

He pictured himself riding in the sidecar with Police Officer Sue and Police Officer Sam at the helm. "Hang on tight, Benny," he imagined them calling as they flew around a tight corner. The wind blew his ears straight back.

Then Benny looked at Rosie who sat beside Fran. He looked at Rosie and Fran together. He felt a tug from his chest, directly to theirs, when he looked at them. He felt something like a powerful magnetic force pulling him to them.

Benny walked to the back of the Perogy Palace

and sat down between Rosie and Fran. Rosie's eyes brimmed with happy tears and she put her arms around Benny. Fran beamed and hugged Benny too.

Everyone clapped. Then they stood up and kept on clapping.

"I won't pretend we're not disappointed," Police Officer Sue said, "but we respect your decision, Benny."

Then Police Officer Sam whispered into Police Officer Sue's ear.

"Why didn't I think of that?" said Officer Sue. She smiled at the attentive audience, then said, "Rosie, Fran, and Benny Bensky, would you consider being Special Agents for the Smith Falls Police Force so we can call you in for special hard-to-crack cases?"

Rosie, Fran, and Benny didn't answer right away. Benny raised an eyebrow as if asking a question.

"Yes, you will each have a cap with your name in gold on the front," Police Officer Sam smiled.

Rosie, Fran, and Benny looked at each other.

"Yes," said Rosie and Fran together. "We'll do it." They gave each other a high five, and Benny thumped his tail against the leg of a chair, making a happy dinging sound.

"Hip-hip, hooray!" the crowd cheered.

"Perogies for everyone!" Mr. Bensky yelled. "On the house!"

A huge ice cream cake covered with sprinkles and smarties and gumdrops was wheeled out by Mrs. Bensky, who was wearing her puffy white perogy costume.

Rosie and Fran had strawberry perogies with lots of sour cream, then they had their cake with double sprinkles, smarties, and gumdrops, the way they liked it. Benny had meaty perogies with lots of butter, then had his ice-cream dropped on the hot front sidewalk and slightly melted, the way he liked it.

"Oh, what a charming restaurant, and such a handsome dog with his own hat!" three ladies with sunglasses said. "We don't have anything like this back in Florida. Can we take a picture? We want to recommend the Perogy Palace to all our friends."

"What a wonderful day," said Mrs. Bensky when the last of the well-wishers had eaten their perogies.

The clock above the door said seven o'clock. It was time to shut off the lights, lock the doors, and go home.

"One more question," called the red-haired reporter, who was still making notes from a table near the door. "I need something snappy to go with your pictures in the *Smith Falls Times*." She turned to Rosie, her pencil and paper in hand. "What was the highlight of your day, Rosie?"

"I'm happy that Benny got pardoned," said Rosie. "I'm happy that Benny can stay in Smith Falls and live with me and my mum and dad."

The red-haired reporter wrote that down.

"I'm happy we got police hats and that we can have more adventures together," Fran grinned. And the reporter wrote that down as well.

"I'm glad the perogies taste like perogies again," said Mrs. Bensky, her face beaming, her perogy costume slightly splattered with ice cream after a long but happy day.

"Make sure you write down that I always said that dog was a genius," Mr. Bensky said. "You got that? G-E-N-E-E-Y-U-S!"

"And you, sir," the red-haired reporter asked, turning to Benny. "What made you the happiest?"

What made him happy? That was easy. Benny knew the answer to that. The pardon made him happy. The gold HERO medal that would soon hang above his dog dish made him happy. The new police hat made him happy too. But what made him the absolute happiest was the same thing that had made him happy since that first day he met Rosie and Fran in the park: he had friends who saw the good in him, the not-so-good, the in-between, and they were – always, forever, no-questions-asked – his best friends anyway.

Benny Bensky jumped up with one paw on Rosie, the other paw on Fran, and gave each of their faces a big slobbery kiss.

Grandma Bensky's Perogy Recipe

Dough:
Mix 2 cups flour, ½ teaspoon salt, ⅔ cup lukewarm water. Knead lightly to make a soft dough that can be rolled. Choose one of the following fillings for your perogies.

Potato-cheese Filling:
Mix 1 cup dry cottage cheese with 1 cup mashed potatoes, a sprinkle of salt, 1 egg yolk (if desired), and 1 chopped onion sautéed in butter.

Sauerkraut Filling:
Squeeze 2 cups sauerkraut to remove liquid. Sauté in butter with 1 chopped onion.

Strawberry Filling:
Sprinkle 1 cup of chopped fresh berries with 1 table-spoon of flour to thicken the juice.

Form walnut-sized balls from the dough. Roll into rounds. To fill perogies, place a spoonful of filling in center of dough, fold over, and press edges to seal. Lay on dry kitchen towel and cover.

To cook, drop stuffed perogies in a large pot of boiling water a few at a time. Boil rapidly for about 4 minutes. Lift out with a slotted spoon and drain.

Coat with melted butter and serve hot with sour cream. Delicious as leftovers, sautéed in butter.